BEAR STORIES

BEAR STORIES

Hubert Evans

Illustrated by Kim LaFave

NIGHTWOOD EDITIONS

NIGHTWOOD EDITIONS
P.O. Box 411
Madeira Park, BC Canada V0N 2H0

Design by Roger Handling
Drawing of Hubert Evans by Robert Jack

Canadian Cataloguing in Publication Data

Evans, Hubert, 1892–1986
    Bear stories

    (The Forest friends series)
    ISBN 0-88971-153-4

    1. Black bear—Juvenile literature.   I. LaFave, Kim.   II. Title.
III. Series: Evans, Hubert, 1892–1986. The forest friends series.
QL737.C27E92 1991   j599.74′446   C91-091677-2

Printed in Canada

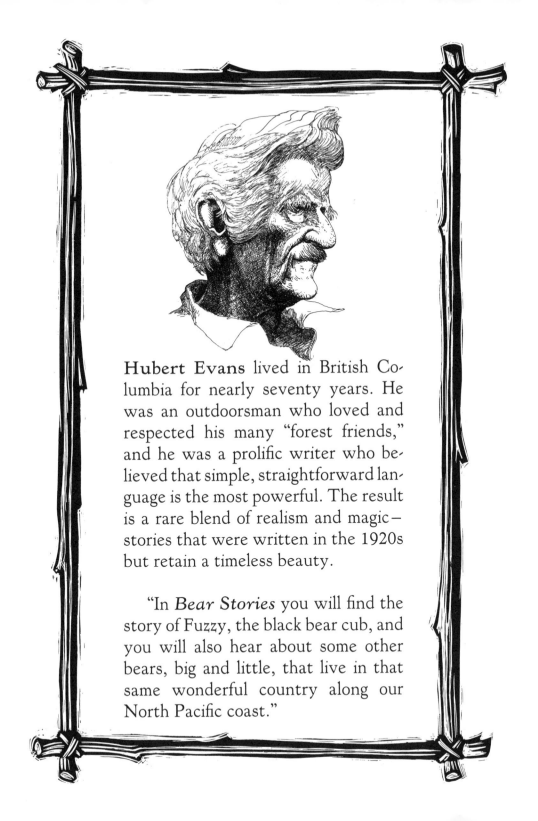

Hubert Evans lived in British Columbia for nearly seventy years. He was an outdoorsman who loved and respected his many "forest friends," and he was a prolific writer who believed that simple, straightforward language is the most powerful. The result is a rare blend of realism and magic — stories that were written in the 1920s but retain a timeless beauty.

"In *Bear Stories* you will find the story of Fuzzy, the black bear cub, and you will also hear about some other bears, big and little, that live in that same wonderful country along our North Pacific coast."

THE FIRST FISH

The black bear came to the river to fish for salmon. And of course Fuzzy, her cub, came with her. For weeks she had fed in the berry patches along the mountainsides. Now she had come to the river for the great feast of the year. When that was over she would seek a den and drowse during the long winter.

Fuzzy had never seen salmon before. Neither had he seen his mother fish for them. So when she made him sit at the edge of the gravel bar he was very interested in seeing how his mother went about catching them.

She waded into the shallow water with the current flowing about her short legs, and stood quite still. Her low growl told Fuzzy not to move. Fuzzy wrinkled his black forehead, stretched his neck and watched.

Minute after minute passed. Still his mother stood in the water without ever moving. In the pool below the narrow channel in which she stood, salmon were swimming restlessly. And the she-bear knew that soon some of them would try to pass upstream through the channel.

Suddenly the
cub saw her paw swing
downward with vicious speed.
She scooped something from the water.
There was a splash, and a writhing shape
thumped to the gravel almost at his feet. He cringed
but did not move from the spot where he had been
told to stay. He wondered what that strange thing
was. His mother waded quickly ashore and sank her
teeth into the rounded back of the salmon, then
carried it a safer distance from the water. There she
ate it. Fuzzy crowded close and licked the cold slime
from the wide tail.

His mother went back to the channel and waited again. She caught two more before it grew dark. When she could no longer see the salmon she came ashore. Fuzzy could hear them splashing over the shallows on their way upstream. But his mother knew that though many would go up the stream that night, others would come to take their places in the pool below her fishing ground. The spawning salmon would pass up in a long procession. And the end of the procession was weeks away. She could catch all the fish she wanted before then.

She took Fuzzy to a bed under the drooping cedar boughs to wait until the dawn came.

FUZZY GOES FISHING

For the first week or so of the fishing season Fuzzy's mother made him sit on the bank. A black bear cub has to learn how to fish, and there is no better way of learning than watching how his mother does it. But by the end of the second week

the old black bear had thrown more salmon out on the gravel bar than she and her cub could eat. There were plenty of salmon in the river. It did not matter much if the cub scared a few. So instead of just watching his mother, Fuzzy at last got a chance to try his hand at the game.

One hot September afternoon his mother slept on the bed under the big cedar at the top of the low bank. So Fuzzy stole out onto the gravel bar with his mind made up to catch a big salmon. His mother always stood in the shallow water and waited for the fish to come within striking distance of her wide paw. The cub tried that. He waited and waited. At first no fish would come near. Then when one did he was not quick enough, or strong enough, to throw it out onto the bar. The fish slithered off his little paw and darted out into deeper water.

Fuzzy frowned and glared at the clear

water as if the water had been to blame for his misfortune.

But soon he grew tired of waiting for fish to come to him. He could not land them when they did. So he would go after the fish. He would show them what a clever cub could do.

Just below where he stood was a little bay in the river bank. He thought that should be a good place to corner these big fish. So he waded in.

But the salmon were too fast for him. They could swim much faster than he could wade with his short little legs. At first he went carefully, but after several salmon had dodged him, he became reckless and tried to rush at them. But he had no better luck than before. The only satisfaction he got was in seeing the big salmon hurry to escape him. If only one would wait until he came within striking distance!

Most of the fish in the little bay went out to the deeper water in the river to wait until this clumsy fisherman went away. But a few refused to leave their spawning grounds in the bay. He chased those back and forth across the shallows. All he did was wet his woolly coat and drench his face with water. It made him very cross.

Then he noticed that when he drove the fish, some of them went in behind a log lying just in the water. Surely he could corner one of those. But no, they all doubled back and avoided him.

He tried that move again. This time they turned back again. All but one. He foolishly tried to wriggle under the log. With a mighty bound Fuzzy jumped for him. He pinned him to the bottom with all his four feet. Then, feeling that the slippery form was going to wriggle free, he plunged his head under water. He put it so deep that even his ears were out of sight and he kept it under for about half a minute. Would he ever be able to hold that salmon with his white little teeth? At last his head popped up. He had it.

That was how Fuzzy caught his first salmon. Later, he learned better ways of fishing. But it is doubtful if he ever got so much satisfaction as when he waded ashore with that first hard-won prize.

THE BEAR AND THE TREE

A hunter was crossing a big beaver meadow, where there were no trees but only long grass higher than his knees. He was about in the middle of the meadow when he saw the head and shoulders of a black bear rise up above the grass. This man

had heard many wild stories about how fierce bears were. He thought he was in great danger. Had he left the bear alone he would have been quite safe. But he thought it would rush at him. So he lifted his rifle and fired. And then he dropped his rifle and ran, for the bear gave a startled grunt and came straight for him. The man was running for the nearest tree, a balsam which stood out a little from the edge of the woods. He ran faster than he had ever run before. But when he was only halfway to

the tree he looked quickly back and saw that the bear was close at his heels. The poor man thought that in a second or two the bear would kill him. He could hear the *thump thump* of the heavy paws behind him. He dodged, but he knew the bear could dodge too. It was all over now, he thought.

When he dodged, the big black form shot past him. But it did not turn back to get him. It bounded straight on until it reached the balsam tree. It climbed to the very top before it looked down to find the man who had frightened it.

It took the amazed hunter some moments to understand that his shot had frightened the bear so badly that its first thought was to climb a tree. And the tree it made for was the same tree the hunter

had been running toward.
He picked up his rifle and
went home, thankful that
bears were not so fierce
as the storytellers had
made him think
they were.

The Bear by the River

We were canoeing down a river near the coast. It was September, and thousands of salmon were spawning there. Away down the river we saw a bear standing on the end of a log which ran out

over the water. As we came downstream we expected him to run from the log and hide in the woods. He did not run though. He went on fishing. We brought the canoe closer and closer until we were only sixty feet from him. Then we held it in the current with the long canoe pole.

The big black fellow stared into the water with his head on one side. Quietly we felt around for the camera. As usual when there was a good picture to be taken, we had left it in camp.

After about five minutes watching, he raised his front paw carefully, scooped it quickly into the water and brought out a salmon. He held it against the side of the log, took it in his mouth and walked into the woods with it. He came back and caught two more. Now and then he would look up at us and then go on fishing. When he had taken his third salmon into the woods he did not return.

Next day we went back to the log with the camera. But we did not get a picture, for the bear had gone.

The Bear Who Waved

Bears are short-sighted. But here is the story of a bear and a short-sighted man.

This man went trolling for trout in the lake. He rowed his boat down one side of the lake where the water was deep enough to fish close to shore. Then at the upper end of the lake there was a swampy stretch, and he had to keep farther out. When he was rowing away from that he looked up. We will let the man tell the rest of his story.

"I looked up," he said, "and I saw what I thought was a man. He was standing beside a high berry bush. He was waving to me. He was wearing a long black coat, and I could see his arm go up as he beckoned for me to come.

I watched, and I saw him beckon again.

"'That's strange,' I said to myself. 'Some poor fellow is lost in the woods. He wants me to rescue him.'

"So I turned the boat around and rowed back for him. Once I looked over my shoulder, and he was still there, waving to me. I rowed faster. When I came close to shore I stopped rowing and turned around to have another look at him. I was so surprised I almost fell out of the boat. It wasn't a man at all. It was a black bear standing on his hind legs and reaching for berries at the top of the bush. As soon as he saw me he crashed away through the brush."

HOUSEBREAKERS

A man and his wife found two bear cubs in the woods. They knew that their mother must have been shot or trapped or she would not have left them. The cubs were hungry and whimpered. So they took them to their cabin. "We fed them from a bottle at first," the man said. "We told ourselves we were going to have a pair of amusing pets.

"They were amusing too. They used to tumble and wrestle with one another, and they came in and out of the house like a couple of puppies. In two months we couldn't go anywhere without having them at our heels. They were interested in everything we did, and they were always getting in our way.

"But I didn't mind that so much," the man went on. "It was the appetites they had. They wanted to eat all the time. One evening I gave them a big supper. But when we had gone to bed they came up to the door and thumped to be let in. They made so much noise we couldn't sleep. We knew they couldn't be very hungry after the big suppers they'd had. So I went out and chased them off the porch. I was hardly back in bed before they were at the

door again. I shouted at them to go away. But they took no notice of that. At last I heard a loud bang and the sound of breaking glass. I went out and found that the brown one had shoved his paw through the window. He had broken the sash as well as the glass.

"I knew we wouldn't get a wink of sleep until they were fed again. So I threw them each a loaf of bread. We couldn't spare the bread. But we wanted some sleep and were willing to pay the bears for it.

"I was glad when the snow came, and they went somewhere to den up for the winter. If they'd stayed much longer they'd have made us poor trying to feed them.

"Before spring we'd left that cabin. I hope they got on all right without us."